For Jack,

Read on.

KOKOPELLI
AND THE

ISLAND OF CHANGE

BY MICHAEL STERNS

Grasshopper
dream
productions

ILLUSTRATED BY ERIK HAGEMAN   LAYOUT BY DUSTIN ROWLEY

Copyright © 2005 by Michael Sterns

Library of Congress Catalog Card Number: 2004117115
ISBN 0-615-12724-X

Printed in China by Everbest Printing Co. Ltd
through Four Colour Imports, Ltd.

Grasshopper Dream Productions
777 Claudia Lane
Palm Harbor, FL 34683

Book orders: www.grasshopperdreams.com
813-382-4230

Sterns, Michael.
   Kokopelli & the island of change / by Michael Sterns
; illustrated by Erik Hageman. -- 4th ed.
   p. cm.
   SUMMARY: Pirates shipwreck on the island where
Kokopelli and his bride Samsara are honeymooning. Over
time the pirates become kinder and shift their focus
from hoarding treasure to treasuring the beauty of
nature, friendship, family, and love.
   Audience: Ages 5-12.
   LCCN 2004117115
   ISBN 0-615-12724-X

   1. Kokopelli (Pueblo deity)--Juvenile fiction.
2. Pirates--Juvenile fiction. 3. Nature--Juvenile fiction.
4. Interpersonal relations--Juvenile fiction.
[1. Kokopelli (Pueblo deity)--Fiction. 2. Pirates--Fiction.
3. Nature--Fiction. 4. Interpersonal relations--
Fiction.]   I. Hageman, Erik. II. Title.

PZ7.S83957Kok 2005   [E]
                    QBI04-800141

Plant & Location: Printed by Everbest Printing (Guangzhou,
China), Co Ltd
Production Date: 07/01/12
Job/Batch Number: 108394

When we last met, fair reader, we learned of a man named Kokopelli who always lived life to the fullest. Kokopelli journeyed far and wide, enjoying nature's amazing scenery as he walked the land.

He loved adventures and discovering, and was always ready to explore. The beauty of the sunsets, mountains, forests, and animals always brought a smile to his face and peace to his heart. Kokopelli befriended and cared deeply for his animal brothers and sisters he met along the way.

Kokopelli's love of Mother Earth inspired him to teach others to care for her. He showed the tribes the importance of keeping the land and water clean, as all people and animals depend on this to live. He also reminded them to be kind to all the animals. Kokopelli helped the people plant trees to keep the forests strong, so the creatures would always have a wonderful and healthy habitat in which to live.

Kokopelli even taught people to care more deeply for each other by working out their problems peacefully. He encouraged them to speak nicely and to listen more, rather than arguing or fighting. His gentleness certainly encouraged others to be kind.

While exploring one day, Kokopelli met a tribe and its cruel chief, who kept a beautiful butterfly in a cage. The butterfly was very sick and scared, and Kokopelli could see that it was dying.

Kokopelli bravely set the butterfly free after outrunning the mean chief and his angry men. All the animals gathered around to watch, and Kokopelli could tell they knew the butterfly and were thankful to him for letting it go.

The next day the animals introduced Kokopelli to their best friend... a kind, gentle woman named Samsara with rainbow colored eyes. She was the butterfly! He then learned that as a child she had lost her family and was raised peacefully by these animals.

The chief found Samsara playing with her wolf brothers and sisters and saw her rainbow colored eyes. He was afraid of her because she looked and acted so differently. He ordered his medicine man to cast a spell upon her, changing Samsara into a butterfly. By changing her into the gentlest of the creatures, he could keep her in a cage and feel safe. Had only the chief talked to Samsara, he would have known that she was a kind, sweet young girl who was just a little different.

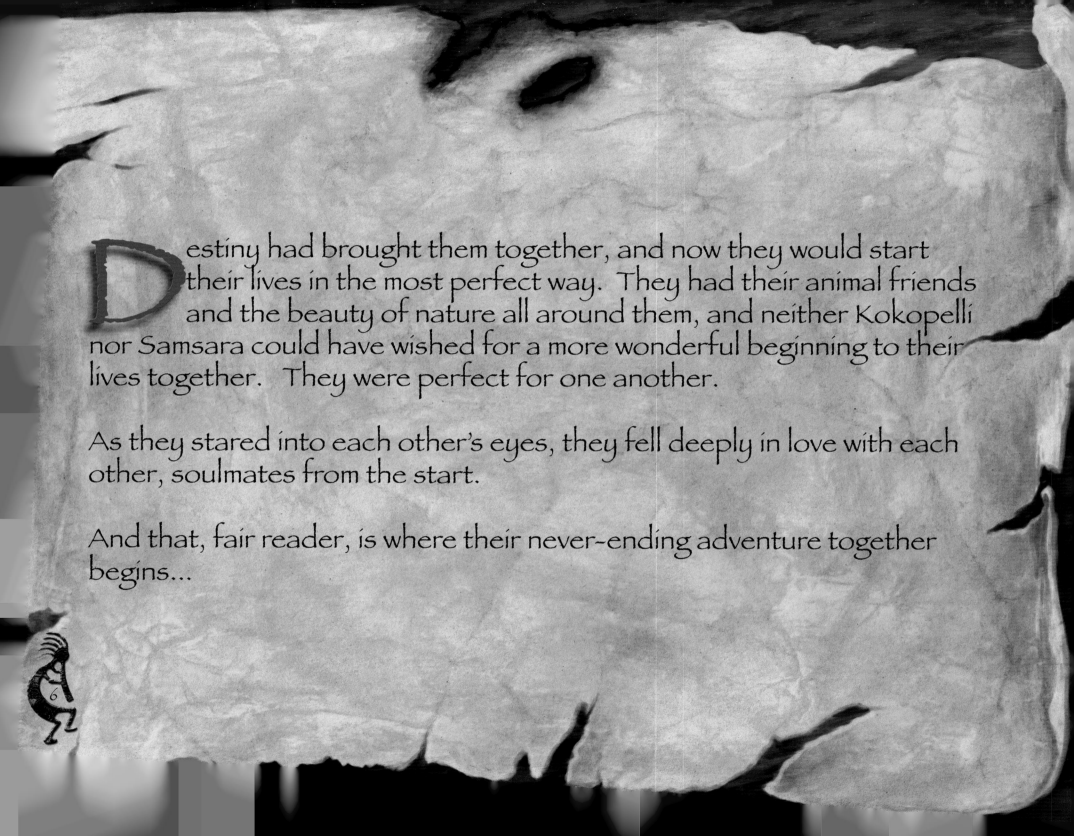

Destiny had brought them together, and now they would start their lives in the most perfect way. They had their animal friends and the beauty of nature all around them, and neither Kokopelli nor Samsara could have wished for a more wonderful beginning to their lives together. They were perfect for one another.

As they stared into each other's eyes, they fell deeply in love with each other, soulmates from the start.

And that, fair reader, is where their never-ending adventure together begins...

Kokopelli and Samsara traveled to far-off lands. They loved meeting and laughing with other people. The happy couple met others from all over the world and felt the color of a person's skin was of no more importance than the color of their eyes.

They delighted in learning about different cultures... eating their fantastic food, wearing their beautiful clothes, and speaking some of their interesting sounding languages. Kokopelli and Samsara learned so much being with people from these distant places, never caring that the other people looked and acted differently.

They were thankful for the constant changes in their lives, and they welcomed the unknown with childlike curiosity. They also learned that with change comes learning and growth. They knew that change is the only thing that always happens, and sometimes change can even be a bit scary.

Kokopelli and Samsara also knew that after every thunderstorm the sun returns like a smile in the sky.

Kokopelli and Samsara explored like this for a long time, and they fell more deeply in love with each other every day.

9

One day Samsara looked at Kokopelli with a concerned expression on her face, and he quietly listened as she told him what was on her mind. She wanted to go back and make peace with the chief who had her turned into a butterfly. It was something she needed to do, and Kokopelli admired her courage.

Chief Sleeping Bear felt badly about what he had done and agreed to speak to Samsara alone. They smiled as they exchanged gifts called peace offerings. Chief Sleeping Bear listened calmly and sadly as Samsara explained how terrible it felt to be transformed into a butterfly and trapped in a cage. She also told him how much more she appreciated her amazing life, never taking one moment for granted.

Chief Sleeping Bear did not interrupt her, knowing he owed her his full attention. When Samsara finished speaking, he explained how he learned from his father and grandfather to fear people who were different . They taught him to be mean to people who didn't look or act the same as he. Samsara understood, and she forgave the chief.

With tears rolling down their cheeks, Chief Sleeping Bear and Samsara hugged each other. The chief promised to teach all who would listen to enjoy the differences between people, and from that day forward he always kept his word.

That night as his heart overflowed with love, Kokopelli asked Samsara if she would marry him. With their eyes full of happy tears she responded, "I would be honored to be your wife, darling Kokopelli." With huge grins upon their faces, they shared the news with the tribe. They asked Chief Sleeping Bear if he would honor them by presiding over the wedding.

After the wedding, the newlyweds and the tribe shared a feast beyond all feasts. The forest was filled with the sounds of drumming, singing, laughing and whoops of delight as they celebrated late into the night. Smiling, the tribe's people fell asleep with the new feeling of hope that forgiveness provides. It was a welcome change for all.

It wasn't long before the newlyweds decided to explore once again, and they soon found the perfect place for a honeymoon. It was a fantastic island, as breathtakingly beautiful as could be.

There were magnificent velvety green mountains covered with lush rain forest. A cool, clear freshwater river flowed through the island. The beaches were made of sugary soft white sand, caressed by the lovely aquamarine colored waters at the shoreline. Gorgeous coconut palm and vine-covered trees, alive with the chatter of the jungle's animals, shaded the edge of the beach.

The island pulsed with the activity of its creatures. Colorful birds called out to each other with their impressive songs. Monkeys of all sorts swung through the canopy of the trees, playing wildly in their branches. Dolphins jumped and splashed in the water just offshore as brilliantly colored crabs scuttled across the sand. Panthers, turtles, lizards and all the other creatures of the island shared their home in harmony with Kokopelli and Samsara.

15

They built a sturdy, tidy hut together, complete with a garden to provide them delicious food. They had a nice fire for cooking and keeping them warm when the nights were cool. Many an evening was spent preparing fantastic meals, while Samsara sang wonderful songs from her childhood. They shared many happy nights together as Kokopelli played his flute and danced to Samsara's singing and drumming.

The couple loved their magnificent island home... but little did they know a big change was coming their way.

In the distance, a pirate ship was sailing toward the peaceful island. It was a very old boat and in terrible shape, with its tattered skull and crossbones flag whipping the air. The sails were torn in many places, and its masts and crows nest sagged under the strain of the wind. The ship's ropes were old and frayed and in danger of snapping. Its wooden planks creaked and groaned as it sailed through the water, and the boat looked as if it might spring a leak at any moment!

The ship sailed low in the water, as if it held a very large load in its belly. It dragged slowly through the waves, with its heavy cargo weighing it down.

There were three brothers on the deck of the ship. The oldest, Captain Dave, was a mean, salty dog of a pirate who had sailed the seven seas for a long, long time. He had a hook at the end of one arm, a peg for one of his legs and a patch over one eye that told the story of his many sea battles. Even his parrot, Uncle Joe, was always crabby and ready for trouble.

The middle brother, Commodore Geoffrey, was a powerful and handsome swashbuckler. He wore the finest clothes and jewelry, and proudly displayed his shiny sword. He was a smooth talker, and prided himself on swindling others out of their treasure. He had a gleam in his eye and certainly had heard his share of roaring cannons.

The youngest brother was Mick, who wasn't a pirate at all. Although he tried hard to be like his older brothers, he just didn't have it in his kind heart to fight or steal. Treasure and piracy held no interest for him, but he was an excellent sailor. He loved to guide the ship like an old friend upon the oceans, among the creatures of the deep. He never tired of the lovely sunsets and the seagulls' songs. He smiled as he listened to the ship's hull cut through the waves, the wind singing through its ropes and sails. The dolphins and whales often added the whooshing of their blowholes to this song as he sailed along.

The two pirates argued fiercely over the huge pile of treasure down in the ship's hold, and how it should be divided. The pirates were so distracted with their squabble that neither of them had their hands on the ship's wheel! Mick was tired of his brothers' endless arguing, so he sat on the bow of the ship to be soothed by the ocean's sounds and views. With Mick and his brothers so distracted, the ship was on a collision course with the island!

20

Down below gleamed a mountain of the finest diamonds, emeralds, rubies, pearls and gold coins imaginable. The pile of treasure was so huge it would take *twenty* lifetimes to spend! The brothers didn't know the hold of the ship also held a surprise.

Sleeping among the treasure were three sisters. Their names were Brandy, Veronica, and Sunny. Brandy was the oldest, had stunning red hair, and watched over her little sisters carefully.

The middle sister Veronica had chestnut brown hair and was the most adventurous of the three. It was her idea to go on this trip.

Sunny was the youngest, and her name described the color of her blond hair and her personality. She was kind and sweet, and loved to explore nature and play with her animal friends.

They had tired of the boring life in their humdrum little village and sneaked aboard the ship the night before. They did this under cover of the darkness, and the brothers did not know they were below. The ladies were eager to share a new adventure in a faraway place. The arguing of the pirates awakened them and, oh, how their lives were about to change!

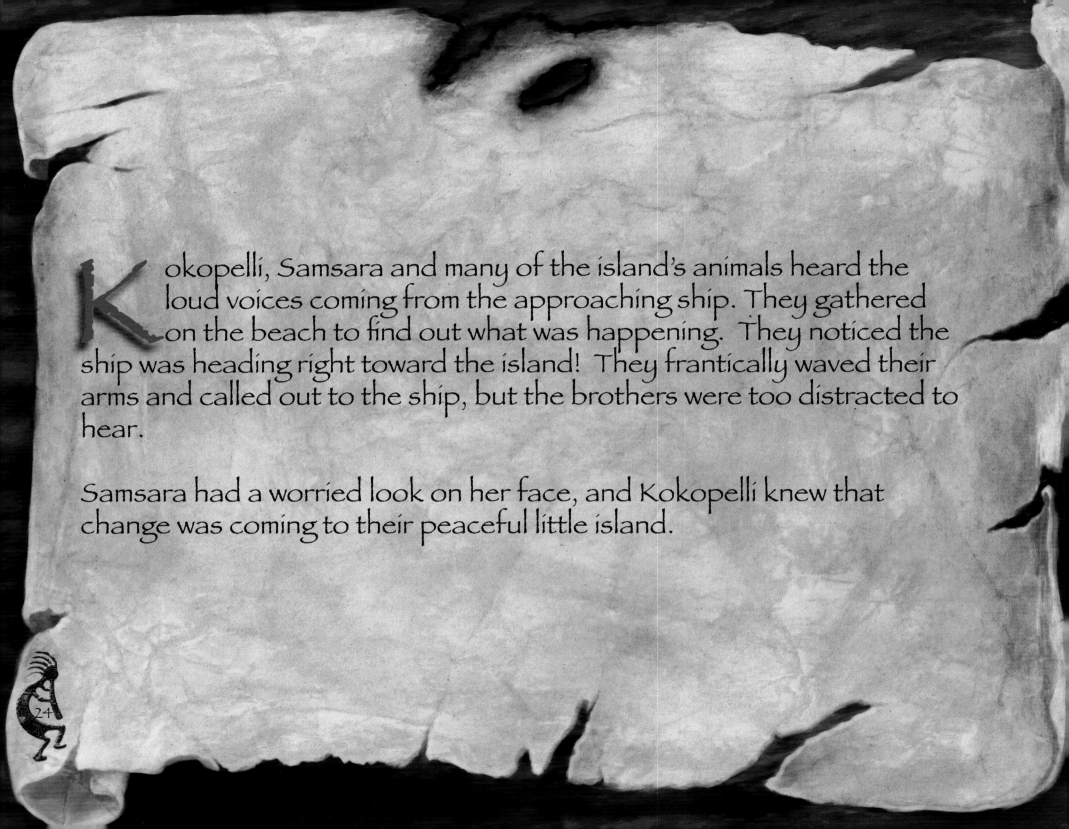

Kokopelli, Samsara and many of the island's animals heard the loud voices coming from the approaching ship. They gathered on the beach to find out what was happening. They noticed the ship was heading right toward the island! They frantically waved their arms and called out to the ship, but the brothers were too distracted to hear.

Samsara had a worried look on her face, and Kokopelli knew that change was coming to their peaceful little island.

Mick continued to daydream on the bow of the ship. He was used to his brothers' arguing, and the ocean's beauty soothed him at times like these. He loved the way the sunlight danced on the rolling blue waves. A smile brightened his face as he heard the familiar sounds of the dolphins' blowholes whooshing as they breathed and jumped. They were so graceful as they frolicked. Mick didn't know they were trying to warn him that his ship was in danger!

"The dolphins are so full of energy today. And what a beautiful sight to see with the island's palm trees swaying in the ocean breeze", Mick sighed. "ISLAND?!!!" he hollered as he jumped up and finally realized what was happening.

With a bone jarring thud and crunch the ship wrecked on the beach, ripping a huge hole in its side.

At that moment everyone's lives would change forever.

Captain Dave and Commodore Geoffrey began yelling even more loudly, this time over whose fault it was they had wrecked. There was no way the ship could sail again in its condition. Instead of planning ahead and making camp, the brothers began the seemingly useless task of unloading the ship's treasure onto the shore. The pirates barked orders at poor Mick, who did all the work as they again argued over which treasure belonged to whom. Even Uncle Joe the parrot squawked loudly, adding to the commotion.

Brandy, Veronica and Sunny climbed off the ship with Kokopelli and Samsara's help. Realizing they were among the treasure the entire time, Mick saw the sisters' frightened expressions. Smiling, Mick looked the other way, pretending not to see. He didn't want his brothers to have something else to fight about. Samsara whisked the sisters to her hut, calming them and learning about their adventure.

With the treasure finally unloaded, the brothers were too tired to build a proper camp or search for food. They sat near the treasure looking miserable and worried. Feeling sorry for them, Kokopelli decided to approach the tired men and invite them over.

The Captain and Commodore immediately drew their swords. As greedy as they were, they assumed Kokopelli was coming over to steal their treasure.

"Come on guys, calm down and let's at least see what he has to say, okay?" Mick asked. They shoved Mick out of the way, and with swords flashing marched toward Kokopelli.

The pirates slashed at him with their swords. Kokopelli gracefully jumped, twisted and spun, dodging the blades he heard slicing the air. With lightning-fast reflexes, Kokopelli easily avoided their weapons and eyed them with an annoyed smile.

Dave and Geoffrey finally stopped, propping themselves up on their swords. They were panting heavily and feeling embarrassed and exhausted, as Kokopelli was too fast for them. Knowing they had met their match, they now listened to his invitation.

"Come now gentlemen, there's no need for that!" Kokopelli said. "All are friendly here. My wife Samsara and I would like to invite you over for a meal to welcome you to the island, that's all! But remember, should you decide to join us, there are three rules on this island: You must keep the land and water clean, you must be kind to the island's animals and people, and you must leave your swords behind."

Kokopelli walked back to his home, flashing a grin at Mick as he passed. Mick smiled back, as he was quite impressed with the way Kokopelli handled his mean brothers.

31

As darkness approached, the brothers rushed to build a shelter, using the ship's sails, ropes and boards. They had no way to start a fire, and the pirates were too proud to ask for help. Mick offered to go ask, and his brothers ordered him to sit down. They shivered as the sun went down and the air cooled.

The Captain and Commodore grumbled as they munched on raw coconuts and smelled the aroma of a delicious dinner cooking on Kokopelli and Samsara's fire. The pirates watched with jealousy, seeing the group laughing and helping each other. They could see comfortable hammocks for the sisters now strung between the palm trees. The older brothers drooled as they watched Kokopelli, Samsara and the sisters devour a delicious stew they cooked together. Mick smiled as he watched the group enjoying themselves, wishing he could join them.

The brothers tried to fall asleep as the last of the sun dropped below the horizon. They were cold, hungry and upset, and as tired as they were it was still hard to fall asleep. They could hear stories being shared by a crackling campfire and secretly longed to share in the fun.

Not even finding comfort in the gorgeous sunset painting the evening sky, Dave and Geoffrey finally fell asleep. Kokopelli, Samsara, Brandy, Veronica and Sunny gathered on the beach to enjoy the beautiful twilight. Mick watched the sky from his camp, feeling soothed by the gorgeous colors.

Kokopelli smiled to himself as he noticed the pile of treasure shining in the last of the sun's rays. None of the brothers realized that the tide began to roll in, slowly washing some of the treasure into the ocean.

The next morning, the brothers awakened to find that Kokopelli had left them a much-needed jug of water while they slept. The men were impressed with Kokopelli's kindness after what happened the night before.

To their surprise, Samsara approached them with a huge platter of food. She also invited them to her village to join in the fun, and reminded the men of the island's only rules. "If you are willing to always keep the land and water clean, and show kindness to the island's animals and people, you are welcome to come over", she said.

"By the way", she said, "remember to leave your swords far behind should you decide to join us!" With that, Samsara went back to her village, leaving them to eat the delicious food she brought.

Mick shouted "Thank you, Samsara!" as she walked away. She smiled, winked and waved back to him. He began to eagerly chomp away at the delicious breakfast, smiling and humming to himself as he ate. The Captain and Commodore proudly waited until Samsara was back in her village before they grabbed and gobbled the food, grunting as they chewed.

That day, the pirates ordered Mick around as they rested lazily in the shade of the jungle's trees. The monkeys and birds chattered at them, obviously annoyed by the men's intrusion.

They hollered at Mick to work on the camp, gather coconuts and to bring supplies from the ship. They told him to "Hurry up!" as their boat was beginning to break apart on the shore. Kokopelli and Samsara looked upset as parts of the ship began to litter the beach.

Soon, the Captain and Commodore fell asleep. Curiously, Mick ventured closer to the friendly village to see what was happening over there. He noticed they were all working together to build a hut for the sisters. Everything looked so neat, organized and wonderful!

Mick felt bad about the litter his ship was creating on the beautiful shore, so he helped Kokopelli and Samsara clean the beach. They picked up every piece of trash the sinking boat created, and soon the beach was as good as new.

Sunny noticed how kind Mick was, and they often talked and smiled at each other. Mick secretly wished he could join Kokopelli, Samsara and the sisters in their friendly village. Mick rushed back to his brothers, noticing they were waking from their naps.

39

That evening, another amazing sunset painted the sky. Mick enjoyed the colors that comforted him in spite of his problems. As he approached his brothers, who were again shivering and munching coconuts, he mustered up the courage to ask them a very important question.

"Why can't we join Kokopelli and Samsara's village?" Mick asked. "It seems so nice over there and everyone is so kind and fun!" He lowered his eyes to watch where his toes were timidly digging in the sand, afraid to meet his brothers' gaze.

His brothers roared with laughter, clutching their ribs and slapping each other on the back as they made fun of him. Geoffrey stood up and began to poke Mick in the chest as he laughed at him, calling him a "Mama's boy" as he towered above him. Backing away, Mick stumbled and fell down, tearing his shirt on a piece of driftwood.

Tears filled his eyes as looked at his torn shirt, his backside smarting from the hard fall. Geoffrey and Dave stood over him, looking uncomfortable as their younger brother began to cry.

"This was my favorite shirt... the one Mom made for me!" Mick hollered furiously as tears fell down his face. He angrily pulled the shirt off and threw it at his brothers, but it sailed over their heads and landed in the sand.

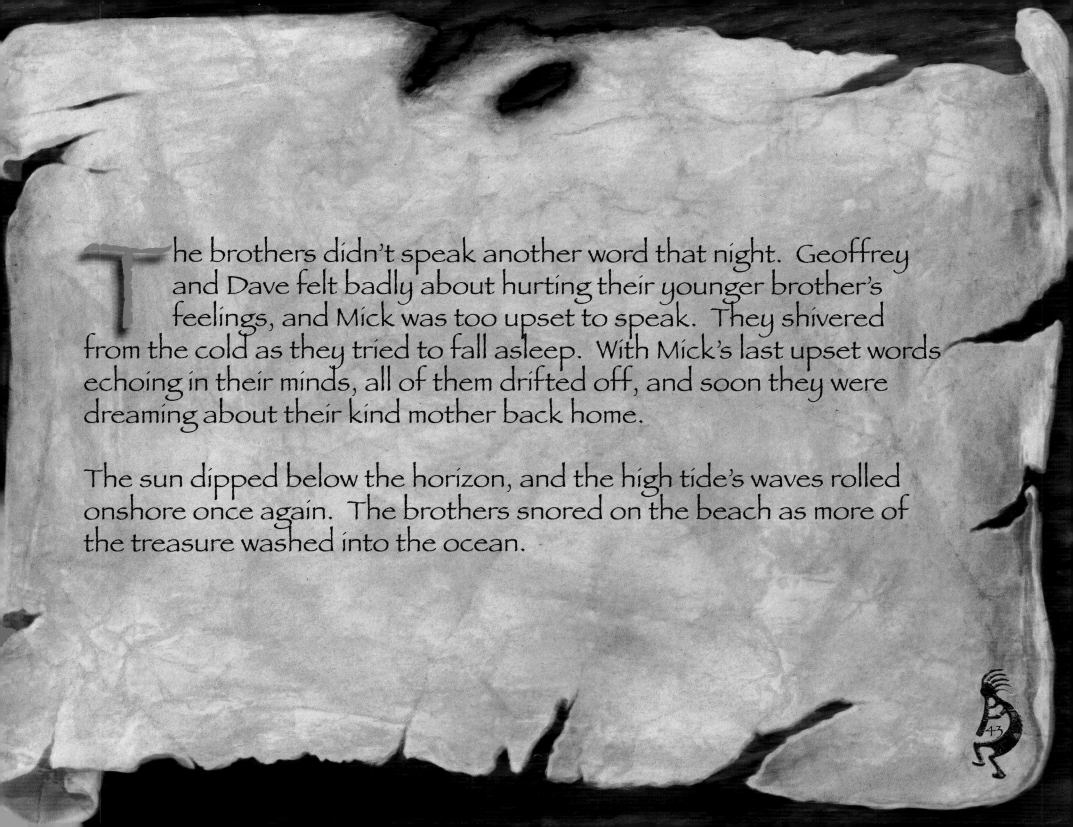

The brothers didn't speak another word that night. Geoffrey and Dave felt badly about hurting their younger brother's feelings, and Mick was too upset to speak. They shivered from the cold as they tried to fall asleep. With Mick's last upset words echoing in their minds, all of them drifted off, and soon they were dreaming about their kind mother back home.

The sun dipped below the horizon, and the high tide's waves rolled onshore once again. The brothers snored on the beach as more of the treasure washed into the ocean.

43

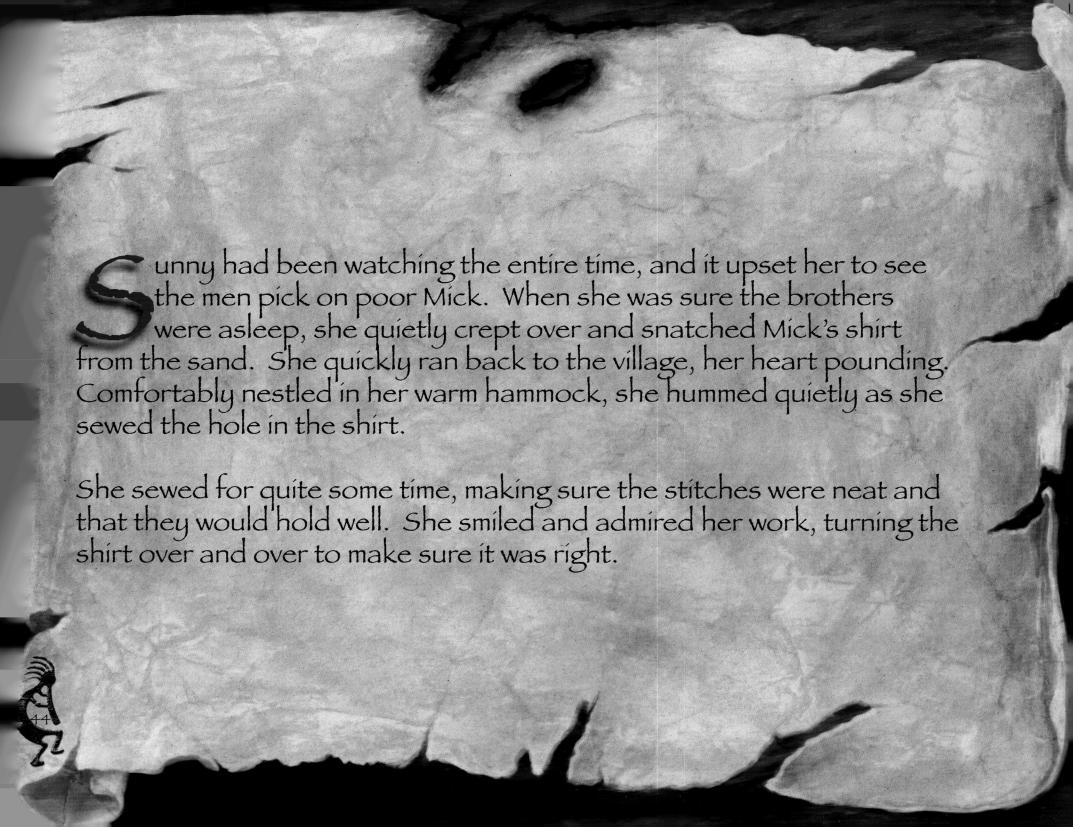

Sunny had been watching the entire time, and it upset her to see the men pick on poor Mick. When she was sure the brothers were asleep, she quietly crept over and snatched Mick's shirt from the sand. She quickly ran back to the village, her heart pounding. Comfortably nestled in her warm hammock, she hummed quietly as she sewed the hole in the shirt.

She sewed for quite some time, making sure the stitches were neat and that they would hold well. She smiled and admired her work, turning the shirt over and over to make sure it was right.

The next morning Mick woke early to greet the day's stunningly beautiful sunrise. Many of the island's animals approached him, as if to say hello and keep him company. He so loved the animals, and they cheered him up as they watched the sun come up together.

As he walked back to his camp, he couldn't believe his eyes. Resting by his pillow was his shirt, neatly folded and wrapped with a palm leaf bow! He untied the bow and looked at his perfectly sewn shirt. He was so happy and surprised, and he looked over to the village. Sunny was stretching and yawning in her hammock, and as she opened her eyes, she and Mick looked at each other.

He proudly held up his shirt and mouthed the words "Thank you" to her. She smiled and waved at him, and mouthed the words "You're welcome."

Just then, Mick made a very important decision. He gathered his few belongings and looked at his brothers with an expression of pity as they snored. He stood up tall and proud and walked over to the village, never once looking back. It was a change he welcomed and needed to make.

The pirates slept for several more hours, and woke up to a surprise. They looked over at Mick's area and found him gone! They didn't see him anywhere, which concerned them because he was always nearby. As they looked around, they noticed a note he left for them scrawled in the sand. It said "NEEDED A CHANGE" in large letters. They looked at each other with their mouths hanging open and eyes wide.

The Captain and Commodore looked over to the village and noticed Mick working with everyone. Mick was smiling and whistling as he helped put the finishing touches on the sisters' hut. They all looked so happy as they worked together, always sharing kind words and smiles.

Captain Dave and Commodore Geoffrey ate their coconuts in silence, and began to miss their little brother's silly ways. Just then, they noticed Kokopelli and Samsara approaching their camp, with another plate of food and jug of water, blankets and some firewood. In Kokopelli's hand was a burning stick, and they knew he was offering them much needed fire.

With welcoming expressions on their faces, the brothers silently invited the pair to join them. Kokopelli taught Geoffrey the best way build a fire, while Samsara taught Dave where plenty of delicious food could be found. The brothers listened intently to the stories of sharing and fun times happening in the growing village. Even Uncle Joe the parrot seemed to smile, as he ate a handful of fruit the couple brought him.

Again Kokopelli and Samsara invited the men to join, reminding them of the island's rules. The men were welcome to join if they promised to take care of the island's land, water, animals and people. And of course, the men were again told they must leave their swords far behind.

For the rest of the day, Commodore Geoffrey and Captain Dave walked around the island separately, taking in the beauty of the mountains, the forest, the animals and the beach. Their eyes and ears were wide open for the first time since arriving on the island, and soon they were smiling.

When they met back at their camp Dave and Geoffrey helped each other prepare a fire and dinner. They complimented each other on the meal and the warmth of the flames.

The men walked to the water's edge, appreciating their first sunset together. They were in awe of the sky's brilliant colors as smiles grew on their faces. The brothers gasped when a dolphin leapt from the ocean, as droplets of water sprayed and sparkled like fantastic diamonds behind it.

As they were about to walk back to their camp, Geoffrey stopped dead in his tracks. "Dave, most of the treasure has washed into the ocean!" he exclaimed.

"You know something, brother? With the wonderful island, animals, people and sunsets we have, I don't need treasure to look at any more. You can have my half of what's left, if you like," Dave said gently.

Geoffrey looked at the jewels and pieces of gold and thought for a moment. Without a word, he turned and walked to the camp and never looked back. Dave turned and followed close behind.

That night the men changed forever, never to be pirates again.

Later in the evening Kokopelli, Samsara, Mick, Sunny, Brandy, and Veronica had a party to celebrate their new friendships and the completion of the sisters' hut. Some of the ladies drummed as Kokopelli danced and played his flute. Mick and Sunny stared sweetly into each other's eyes. They ate, talked and laughed around the fire until late into the night as the animals gathered around to share in the warmth.

Dave and Geoffrey sat around their fire and talked about the fun times they all had as children. They spoke of the fantastic voyages enjoyed together sailing on the ocean. They also remembered how many smiles Mick had brought to their faces throughout the years. Dave and Geoffrey missed their brother Mick, and hoped for a change so they could see him again soon.

That night everyone slept soundly, warmly snuggled in their blankets and with happiness in their hearts.

The next day everyone from the village decided to have a picnic on the beach. They thought it would be fun to have a swim first, to work up a good appetite. They laughed as they played in the ocean, splashing each other in the waves. As they swam, dolphins jumped overhead, pelicans swooped and dove, crabs scuttled, and even the monkeys frolicked on the shore.

Geoffrey and Dave couldn't help but hear the fun, so they decided to sit nearby and watch. They were still a little embarrassed to approach until everyone in the water waved at them and hollered for them to come over. They ran toward the sea like a couple of kids, grinning ear to ear. Geoffrey even showed off with a fancy somersault as he jumped into the water!

Smiling, Dave and Geoffrey called Mick over. He swam to them as fast as he could. They hugged each other, laughed and tousled each other's hair as they played in the ocean. Enjoying a good old splash fight, they all thought back to the days of childhood when they used to do this very same thing together.

56

D ave and Geoffrey were invited to the picnic, and everyone had
a fantastic time. Kokopelli and Samsara smiled as they looked
around. They could see that Mick and Sunny were falling
deeply in love. They saw Geoffrey telling grand stories of life on the
sea, as Veronica listened closely, her eyes as wide as her smile. Dave
was kindly offering Brandy some food, listening politely as she talked.
She was telling him how her dreams of a change from her sleepy village
life had come true.

Kokopelli and Samsara looked deeply into each other's eyes, and felt
powerful love deep in their hearts.

"I love our little island of change," Samsara whispered into Kokopelli's
ear, her head resting on his shoulder. "Me too," he whispered back as
he looked lovingly into her eyes.

A long time passed since that ship wrecked on the Island of Change. Everyone lived together in harmony. They always remembered their promise to care for the land, water, animals and each other. They all shared many wonderful times, and love was all around.

It seems, unlike most people, they all learned to welcome the changes that came their way. Because of this, happiness bloomed in their lives like a sunny meadow of flowers after a Spring rainshower .

They always communicated kindly with each other. They worked their problems out by talking them over peacefully and remembered to listen well. Although the brothers still occasionally argued, it was never as often or fierce as before and never lasted long. They always forgave each other and welcomed the lessons they learned through these disagreements.

Kokopelli and Samsara presided over three weddings on the Island of Change, and never was there a more peaceful community on Earth. Worry and regret were far behind them now as they lived life to its fullest, caught up like playful children in each delightful moment.

By the way, Dave and Geoffrey did of course leave their swords far behind.

With the pirate life left in the past, they didn't even notice when the last of the treasure washed into the ocean.

Of course, everyone lived happily ever after on the Island of Change... could *you*